ROSE'S RED BOOTS

To Ella, Abby and Dave – my darlings. MF

For Amelia, Claire and Shiny. KE

Published in Australia 2017.
First published in the UK in 2018
byNew Frontier Publishing Europe Ltd
93 Harbord Street, London SW6 6PN
www.newfrontierpublishing.co.uk

ISBN: 978-1-912076-97-0 (PB)

Text copyright © Maura Finn 2017
Illustrations copyright © Karen Erasmus 2017
The rights of Maura Finn to be identified as the author and Karen Erasmus to be identified as the
illustrator of this work have been asserted.

A CIP catalogue record for this book is available from
the British Library.

Designed by Celeste Hulme

Printed in China
10 9 8 7 6 5 4 3 2 1

ROSE'S RED BOOTS

Maura Finn
Illustrated by Karen Erasmus

NEW FRONTIER
PUBLISHING

When Rose and Banjo started out the day was bright and new,
The clouds small puffs of fairy floss against the dazzling blue.
A gentle breeze brushed through the trees and made their branches sway.
And ...

The little red boots went marching, marching, marching.
The little red boots went marching
Merrily on their way.

They crossed the stream and meadow where the playful rabbits run,
And buttercups all turn their heads to greet the morning sun.
Beneath the trees the autumn leaves lay scattered on the ground.
So ...

The little red boots went crunching, crunching, crunching.
The little red boots went crunching
To hear that crunching sound.

High up the steepest hill they trooped but when they reached halfway
Banjo turned around, deciding it was time to play.
He raced below, with kite in tow, instead of going up!
So...

The little red boots went chasing, chasing, chasing.
The little red boots went chasing
To catch the cheeky pup.

Naughty Banjo bounded off towards a muddy puddle,
Then tripped, and slipped, and slid, before he plopped down in the middle.
Great muddy paws and dribbly jaws, with all his mischief done.
So ...

The little red boots went splashing, splashing, splashing.
The little red boots went splashing
Because it's *so* much fun!

At last the kite was ready and it leaped high off the ground.
It spun, and spiralled, looped the loop, and zig-zagged all around,
Its ribboned tail a whistling trail of colour speeding by.
And ...

The little red boots went dancing, dancing, dancing.
The little red boots went dancing
Under the broad blue sky.

But ...
       The clouds began to thicken, and the blue sky turned to grey.
     The wind whipped fast and furious as it ripped the kite away.
Tossed through the sky, then way up high, the kite came to a stop.
So ...

The little red boots went climbing, climbing, climbing.
The little red boots went climbing
All the way to the top.

Then all at once the rain clouds burst and thunder boomed on high.
Knives of lightning, piercing, frightening, flashed across the sky.
Poor Rose and Banjo found themselves as soggy as can be.
So ...

The little red boots went racing, racing, racing.
The little red boots went racing ...

home for morning tea.